GW00866781

Little Owl
Leaves the Nest

STORY BY MARCIA LEONARD · PICTURES BY CAROL NEWSOM

A Packard/Montgomery Book

BANTAM BOOKS
TORONTO · NEW YORK · LONDON · SYDNEY

For my parents, who built a fine nest.
— M.L.

RL1, IL 003–006

LITTLE OWL LEAVES THE NEST
A Bantam Book/May 1984

CHOOSE YOUR OWN ADVENTURE® is a registered trademark of
Bantam Books, Inc.
Registered in U.S. Patent and Trademark Office and elsewhere.

Original conception of Edward Packard

Produced by Cloverdale Press Inc.,
133 Fifth Avenue, New York, NY 10003

ISBN 0-553-15266-1

Published simultaneously in the United States and Canada

Bantam Books are published by Bantam Books, Inc. Its trademark, consisting of
the words "Bantam Books" and the portrayal of a rooster, is Registered in U.S.
Patent and Trademark Office and in other countries. Marca Registrada. Bantam
Books, Inc., 666 Fifth Avenue, New York, New York 10103.

PRINTED IN THE UNITED STATES OF AMERICA

0 9 8 7 6 5 4 3 2 1

YOUR FIRST ADVENTURE™

A CONCEPT TO GROW WITH

How to use this book:
When you read Your First Adventure aloud to young
children, start with page two. This will set the scene and
create a "let's pretend" mood. Then read page three,
follow either of the two choices, and continue
the story to its happy ending.

And this is just the beginning . . .
When children are ready for more challenging reading,
there are other levels of CHOOSE YOUR OWN ADVENTURE
waiting for them. Ask your local bookseller.

Pretend you are a little owl and you live in a cosy nest in a big maple tree. One day a blue balloon gets caught in the branches of your tree. You really want that balloon! But you can't fly to get it because you don't know how.

2

Maybe you can walk along the branches to reach the balloon. Or maybe your friend Squirrel will help you get it.

If you want to get the balloon on your own, turn to page 4.

If you want to ask Squirrel to help you, turn to page 10.

3

Off you go to get the balloon.
Is that it behind the leaves?

4

No. That's one of Robin's eggs.
And here she comes now.

"What do you think you're doing?" asks Robin.

"I was looking for a blue balloon," you say. "But I found blue eggs instead."

6

"There's the balloon," says Robin.
And she shows you the way.

7

You tug and tug on the string.

8

OOPS!
Suddenly you're falling.

Turn to page 17.

9

Squirrel's nest looks empty.
"Now who will help me get the
balloon?" you ask.

"I will," says Squirrel.

11

Squirrel leaps from branch to branch. "Follow me," he calls.

"I can't jump that far," you say.

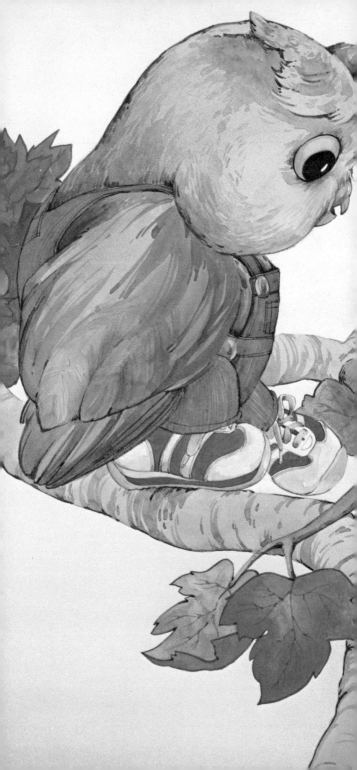

"Then I'll make a bridge," says
Squirrel.

13

Squirrel untangles the string.
"Here's the balloon," he says.

OOPS!
Suddenly you're falling.

You flap your wings as hard as you can. Then you're soaring through the air. You can fly!

And you fly back to your cosy nest with the beautiful blue balloon.

18